_Woody Woodpecker_

# THE PIRATE TREASURE

Library of Congress Cataloging in Publication Data

Lantz, Walter.
  Woody Woodpecker.

  SUMMARY: Splinter and Knothead visit their Uncle
Woody and become involved in a search for buried treasure.
  [1. Woodpeckers—Fiction.  2. Pirates—Fiction.
3. Buried treasure—Fiction]  I. Title.  II. Title:
The pirate treasure.
PZ7.L295Wo5      [E]      77-1611
ISBN 0-307-10505-9

# Walter Lantz ®
## Woody Woodpecker ®
# THE PIRATE TREASURE

gb **GOLDEN PRESS**
Western Publishing Company, Inc.
Racine, Wisconsin

"I can't wait to see Woody again," said Splinter. She and Knothead had come to spend their vacation in the small seaside village, where Woody managed a restaurant just next door to a little theater.

"It looks as if he has lots of customers," said Knothead. "They must be the old sailors and actors Woody wrote to us about."

They waited outside until the last customer left. Woody was straightening up the restaurant and didn't see them enter.

Knothead put his fingers to his lips and tiptoed up behind Woody. Splinter followed. Together they shouted, "Surprise!"

Woody spun around. "Knothead!" he exclaimed. "And Splinter! You finally arrived!" Woody hugged them both. "This calls for a celebration. I think I'll close up the place and just have fun with you. I ran out of fish this afternoon, and I have to wait for a new catch, anyway."

As he spoke, Woody picked up some scrolls that were scattered about the room.

"What are those?" Knothead asked.

"Just a lot of treasure maps the old sailors leave around every day," Woody replied. "Nothing important."

"What do you mean?" exclaimed Knothead. "Treasure maps are always important!"

"Well, the old sailors who come here certainly believe in the stories about buried treasure. They're always drawing up these maps," said Woody. As he dropped the maps into a chest, he added, "They have too much imagination, that's all!"

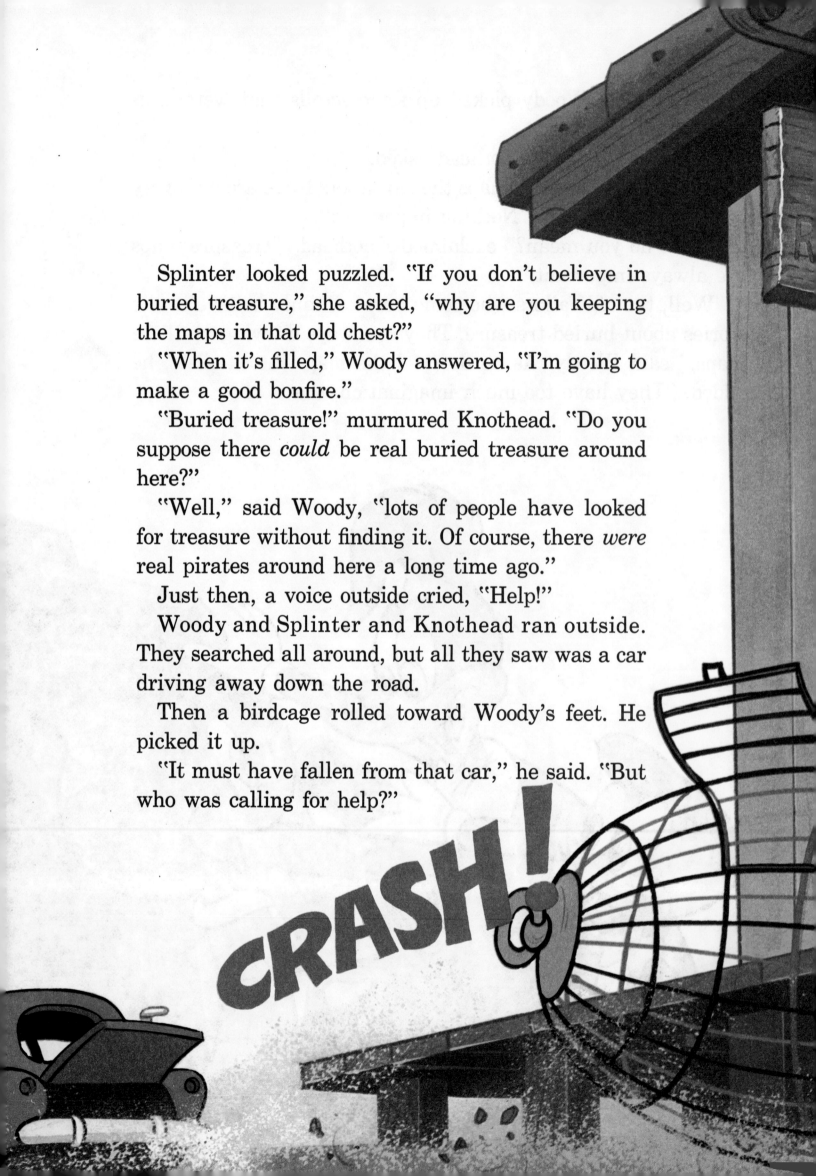

Splinter looked puzzled. "If you don't believe in buried treasure," she asked, "why are you keeping the maps in that old chest?"

"When it's filled," Woody answered, "I'm going to make a good bonfire."

"Buried treasure!" murmured Knothead. "Do you suppose there *could* be real buried treasure around here?"

"Well," said Woody, "lots of people have looked for treasure without finding it. Of course, there *were* real pirates around here a long time ago."

Just then, a voice outside cried, "Help!"

Woody and Splinter and Knothead ran outside. They searched all around, but all they saw was a car driving away down the road.

Then a birdcage rolled toward Woody's feet. He picked it up.

"It must have fallen from that car," he said. "But who was calling for help?"

CRASH!

All three looked around, saw nothing else unusual, and went back inside.

"We'll keep the cage here in the restaurant," said Woody, "just in case the owner returns."

Suddenly someone pounded loudly on the door.

Opening the door, Woody found himself face-to-face with a scowling man who looked like a pirate. "Have you seen a parrot around here?" growled the man.

"No," Woody answered, "but we did find a birdcage, and we heard someone call for help a few minutes ago."

Roughly the pirate pushed Woody aside and entered the room. He looked around. "That parrot *has* to be here!" he snarled. He began searching the restaurant.

Splinter and Knothead were frightened. "What a mean-looking man!" Splinter whispered.

Woody was a little frightened, too, but he spoke up bravely. "Probably the parrot flew away when his cage fell."

"Maybe," sneered the pirate, "and maybe not!" He continued his search. Woody, Splinter, and Knothead watched him in growing alarm.

Finally, the pirate gave up his search and stomped out.

"Whew, that fellow belongs in a history book!" said Woody. "He's as bad as Blackbeard and Captain Kidd and the other pirates!"

The three had not yet recovered from *that* surprise visit, when a parrot, also dressed as a pirate, suddenly appeared. "Ahoy!" he shouted. "Did that old windbag finally leave?"

Woody and the children stared at the parrot, hardly believing what they saw and heard.

Woody said, "*You* must be the parrot the tough pirate was looking for!"

"How did you get in here?" asked Knothead and Splinter at the same time.

"I flew in through the chimney, of course," answered the parrot. "That mean pirate has been keeping me a prisoner backstage in the little theater next door. He finally moved my cage to the trunk of his car. I escaped when the trunk flew open as the car hit a bump in front of your restaurant.

"If you'll protect me from the pirate," he said anxiously, "I'll show you a real treasure map that will lead us all to a fortune in gold!"

"A fortune in gold!" echoed Knothead.

"A *real* treasure map!" Woody exclaimed.

The parrot added, "We'll have to move fast, though, because the pirate already knows the way to the cave where the gold is. He says the ghost of Iron Hook, the pirate, told him the way."

The parrot lowered his voice. "He said that Iron Hook's ghost guards the treasure!"

Woody looked at the parrot doubtfully. "If the pirate knows where the treasure is, why does he need you and the map?"

"He kept me prisoner so I couldn't tell anyone else about the map," explained the parrot. "He kept the map in the trunk of the car, and I reached through the cage bars and grabbed it."

A face appeared at the window, but no one noticed. It was the scowling pirate, and he seemed to be listening to every word!

"Let's go!" cried Woody. "Let's beat that pirate to the treasure!"

"But, Woody," Knothead reminded him, "what if the ghost of Iron Hook *is* guarding the gold?"

"I don't believe in ghosts. We're going to look for the gold," said Woody. "Come on, everybody!"

Meanwhile, the mean-looking pirate, who had smiled after hearing everything they said as he stood by the window, ran down toward the sea. There he climbed into an old rowboat and began rowing mightily.

"I'll get to the cave before they do," he said aloud. He kept rowing until he reached a cave almost invisible among the rocks. After hiding the boat behind a huge rock, he waded through to the dry part of the cave.

A short time later, another boat appeared, also headed toward the cave. With the parrot guiding him, Woody rowed tirelessly, filled with enthusiasm over the treasure hunt.

"Just think!" he said to the children. "Real buried treasure!" He turned to the parrot and asked, "Are we getting close?"

"Yes, just keep rowing," the parrot replied. "We're almost there now."

At last they reached the spot marked on the map. "I see dry land inside that cave," said Splinter, pointing.

"There's no sign of that pirate's boat," Woody said.

"Good!" answered the parrot. "That means we got here first— I hope!"

Woody held his lantern high as they walked along inside the cave. Suddenly the light flickered, leaving them in almost total darkness. "Yikes!" cried Woody nervously.

But then, just as suddenly, the lantern light glowed brightly again. "Our lantern's not out!" exclaimed Knothead with relief.

"Calm down!" advised Woody. "I see a light ahead. You know, this is just like being in a scary play."

Holding their breath, they all walked cautiously toward the light in the distance.

Then they saw it—a huge treasure chest!

"Look!" shouted Woody. "There's the chest of gold!"

"And there's a light! Careful!" warned the parrot. "There's something strange about all this."

Just then a billowy white figure loomed up from behind the chest. Splinter gasped. Knothead cried out, "Iron Hook's ghost!"

"Nonsense!" said Woody. "*I* don't see any ghost." His eyes were on the treasure chest. "All I see is a big chest of gold!" He ran toward it.

A thundering voice roared, "Hah! You have come to steal Iron Hook's treasure!"

Woody stopped in his tracks. "It's the ghost!" he cried.

Woody, Splinter, and Knothead ran toward the cave exit.
"Wait! Ow! Ouch!" wailed a voice behind them.

They looked back and saw the pirate carrying the parrot and limping. Another man, a stranger, was helping him along.

"I tripped over the ghost costume I was wearing," said the pirate. "Ohhh, my leg hurts! I fell over that heavy treasure chest!"

"I'm the director of a new play that's opening soon at the little theater," explained the stranger. "These two are actors. We got you into this to find out how convincing our acting could be, but we didn't really mean to frighten you."

Later, on their way back to the restaurant, Woody, Splinter, and Knothead laughed about their adventure.

"Now I *will* make a bonfire of all those maps," Woody said.

"All except *this* one," said Knothead, holding the map the parrot had given them. "Let's keep it as a souvenir of our great treasure hunt!"